Baba Didi and the Godwits Fly
First published in 2013 by
New Internationalist Publications Ltd
55 Rectory Road
Oxford OX4 1BW
UK
newint.org

New Internationalist New Zealand/Aotearoa
PO Box 35 038
Christchurch 8030

Illustrations by Annie Hayward.

Design: Andrew Kokotka
Editor: Chris Brazier

Printed by 1010 Printing International Limited, Hong Kong, who hold environmental
accreditation ISO 14001.

British Library Cataloguing-in-Publication Data
A catalogue record for this book is available from the British Library.

Library of Congress Cataloging-in-Publication Data
A catalog record for this book is available from the Library of Congress.

ISBN 978-1-78026-130-0

Baba Didi and the Godwits Fly

Written by **Nicola Muir**
Illustrated by **Annie Hayward**
Foreword by
Helen Clark

Foreword

The godwit is indeed a traveller of the world. Among the countries it calls home are the United States, Russia, China, Korea, Japan, Australia, and New Zealand. This small, unassuming bird is truly a global citizen.

The bar-tailed godwit or Kuaka starts its journey on the shores of New Zealand – Ruakaka, Ohiwa and Farewell Spit, and the Firth of Thames. At the end of the Southern Hemisphere summer, the godwits set out on an extraordinary flight across the Pacific Ocean – to the Yalu Jiang reserve in China, where they rest for a few days before flying to their Siberian or Alaskan breeding grounds.

In the Arctic autumn, with the nesting season over and the cold weather closing in, the godwit turns again to the south. In early September, at the global ecological crossroads where Russia and America almost touch, the godwits gather before their non-stop flight back to the other end of the globe. Here, the bar-tailed godwits, heading for the Antipodes, mingle with the Hudsonian godwits preparing for their flight to Tierra del Fuego in Argentina.

There is still so much we don't know about these incredible birds. What indication for flight do they wait for? An alignment of stars? An inner compass that waits for global positioning? A certain temperature? What we do know is that this land-based bird, with no ability to feed or rest on the sea, heads into the wind and flies 11,680 kilometres non-stop across an entire ocean, arriving in little over a week in New Zealand or, for some Australia.

It is little surprise, therefore, that this bird has become for many a symbol of quiet self-assurance and resilience under adversity. What makes the godwits so fascinating is not only that they are shared among so many nations, but also that they have developed an enormous migratory range.

Godwits rely on the marginal lands of estuaries and shorelines, which are rapidly being reclaimed by growing nations. How then will the godwit be affected by climate change and rising sea levels, which may accelerate habitat loss in the years to come? What will become of the rich feeding grounds on which they are so dependent? Will the same conditions that make people leave their homes spell an end to the long flights of the godwit, or will they adapt again to a changed world?

Each year millions of people are forced to leave their homes because of natural disasters or civil unrest, becoming refugees or internally displaced. The resilience they need to reach safety, cross oceans, and then rebuild their lives in new lands can be an inspiration to us. Yet refugees are often marginalized and treated poorly.

Part of my work as head of the United Nations Development Programme is to support the building of resilient communities which mitigate the conditions which cause people to flee their homes. Now, more than ever, we are a global community. Let those of us who are well housed and well connected be part of the global community of care for those who have had to leave everything they know and love behind.

A truly vibrant village of the globe will also allow the flora and fauna we share it with to flourish. Without care and protection of their habitats now, like the remarkable flight of the godwit, they will be part of our past, and not of our future. It is to the godwit that I dedicate these few words.

Helen Clark
Former Prime Minister of New Zealand, now Administrator of the United Nations Development Programme

Nicola Muir lives in Whangarei, in the north of New Zealand/Aotearoa, with Maya and Rodolfo: the best long-distance flying companions ever.

scrubbuzz.com

To Annemarie Florian: thanks!

Thanks to Keith Woodley for his book *Godwits: Long Haul Champions* and for his work at the Miranda Shorebird Centre.

Annie Hayward migrated to New Zealand at 14 and now lives and works in the seaside village of Eastbourne. Lozenges of light and colour reflect the things she loves and collects: blues and greens of sea-glass, the red carpet of fallen pohutukawa flowers and the honey-amber of bunny tail sea grass. She paints to give hope and comfort and many of her figures echo the Madonna/Papatuanuku/Pachamama, a symbol of loving protection and kindness. For many, an Annie Hayward painting is a talisman of love and light when the road is rough and the way is long.

anniehaywardart.co.nz

UNICEF receives royalties from each sale of *Baba Didi and the Godwits Fly*.

UNICEF (UN Children's Fund) works to make the world a better place for children. We believe every child is important and has the right to a happy, healthy and safe childhood. To help kids survive and thrive, UNICEF ensures they have access to their basics needs such as nutritious food, health services and education.

We believe that all of us can make a difference to a child's life – by purchasing this book you are helping children access clean drinking water, get immunized against disease and attend school. Thank you.

For more information about UNICEF please visit www.unicef.org

About the **New Internationalist**
We are an independent, not-for-profit publishing co-operative, and we're not afraid to tell the stories that the mainstream media sidesteps, nor to be the platform for the people living those stories. Our award-winning magazine, books and website provide fresh, hard-hitting, grassroots coverage from voices across the globe.

newint.org

'Look, little one,' said Baba Didi. 'The godwits are getting round and fat like me, getting ready to fly, eating all this good food by the sea.' Pipis, big and juicy, clicked as they fell into the basket.

'Are you getting ready to fly too, Baba Didi?' Isabella grinned, cheeky.

'I could be!' Baba Didi flapped her arms and ran along the sandbank with her dodgy hip; Isabella ran behind her.

'Where are they going?' asked Isabella.

'Round the world! From New Zealand, from this bank here at Ruakaka, Ahipara, from Miranda, Motueka and Farewell Spit, the godwits will one day smell winter, point their long beaks into the wind and they will… go. To Korea, to Japan and China, then to Russia and Alaska to find another summer full of good things to eat.'

'They don't look so amazing.'

'You're not really looking. You watch too many movies, Isabella. Life's not all unicorns and cupcakes, all magic spells and happy ever afters. When you look and see only a small brown bird – you're only looking with your eyes.'

'How else do you look?'

'There are a thousand ways – it depends what you're looking for.'

Isabella still saw just a plain brown bird.

'Look harder. Imagine that bird, flying, flying, sometimes quite alone, over ocean swells as big as mountains, in freezing cold, in hail, in blinding sun. Then you will see it.'

'See what?' thought Isabella and looked hard at her Baba Didi.

'Resilience,' said Baba Didi.

What's that? thought Isabella.

'That means "keep goingness",' said Baba Didi, as if she could hear what the girl was thinking. 'Even when things are really hard.

'At first, you think it's all about Beauty and Talent. Beauty queens and talent shows! Where did that get anyone? Where did that get the peacock? Or the parrot? Mmm? A walled garden and a pirate's shoulder that's where. There's only so far that beauty and talent can take you. Beauty can become a prison; Talent can make you a slave.

'If you're born a peacock, show your feathers. A parrot? Strut your stuff! But that's only half the story. An easy life is not always a gift. If you are born with godwit luck then you will have a long way to fly but you will also find that you have the right wings to keep going till you get to the end.'

Isabella couldn't see any parrots – or peacocks. 'Well…
that's what we all do. Everyone just keeps going till they get
there, don't they?' she said.

'You'd be surprised. It takes a lot to keep going when you're
out of sight of land and there's no one to tell you that you're
going the right way. You need courage. Stamina. A little faith.
It's not about who gets there first – that's for sports and
movies. Mostly what counts in real life is getting there at all.'

'Well, why don't they just stay here like the other birds?'
asked the little girl. 'It'd be more comfortable. Why do **they**
have to be the ones with such a long hard way to fly?' '

Baba Didi looked hard at Isabella. 'When there are hard times, Isabella – everyone always asks, "Why me?" Sometimes you just have to go. Sometimes you just know.

'The godwit knows. Your Poppa and I knew when we left Croatia. Sometimes, if you stay in the same place doing the same thing, it will be the end of you.'

'Anyway – there are many treasures the godwit will see that the other birds will never know.'

'Like what?' asked Isabella.

'Well, like strange and beautiful lands, rich places to feed, volcanoes erupting at sea – you never know what you are going to find when you set out. The godwit is not interested in being comfortable. Comfortable is for peacocks and parrots.

'Your Poppa and I weren't the first ones to come from the old country. Lots of people have come here looking for gold. We're not so different from the godwits. They poke their long fluted beak into the sand looking for godwit gold – the juicy sea worms and crabs that will make them fat enough to fly over an entire ocean.'

'The first people came here in their long canoes looking for a new land. They set out not knowing what was on the other side of the sea, navigating by the stars, guided by courage and good faith. By looking at the birds and the currents, they found what they knew should be here waiting for them: a new land, a new home.

'Our people crossed an ocean and went looking for gold too.'

'Did they find it?'

'No,' said Baba Didi. 'You needed a licence to look for gold and some of them didn't even have money for that.'

'But they went over the burnt ground after all the kauri trees had been cut down, poking their long iron sticks, like godwit beaks, into the earth and do you know what they found?'

'Gold?' guessed Isabella.

'No. Kauri gum. Amber. Tree sap; like little golden bubbles. The ancient kauri wept tears of sap and they dripped down and turned to stone.

'The people didn't know when they left their old country what they'd find. What they found was cold. Hard. Sometimes they went hungry.

'But they kept going and then they found the amber. With the amber they bought land that no one else wanted. Land

that was no good for cows. Did they cry? Did they give up?

'Hard times, Isabella. Hard times are to make all the others give up. For us and the godwit, hard times are just the way to something much better.'

Sometimes Baba Didi's words were hard to follow, thought Isabella.

'What did they do with the land, then?'

'They made wine! It all depends on how you look at things. If you want to farm cows – well, then it might look like hungry land. But if you ask "what is it good for?" then you'll see something different. Grapes like that kind of land! Hah! With the right kind of eyes you can see something good that no one else has seen yet.'

Isabella looked again at the little brown birds.
'How can such a little bird go such a very long way?'
'Well, a godwit can't fly far with a thousand
worries on her wings. She shakes them off and,
instead of being preoccupied, she gets occupied.'
'What is "occupied"?' asked Isabella.

'It means, instead of getting dizzy with all the "what ifs", she gets busy with the "hows". It means she practises a little flying first. She gets a strong heart and a calm mind,' said Baba Didi.

'And a tummy full of seafood?' asked Isabella.

'Exactly,' said her grandmother, laughing. 'But even more important than that, she learns a very special skill. Something that only godwits and old birds like me know about.'

'What is it?' asked Isabella.

'She learns to rest on the wing. She learns not to listen to her mind telling her she is tired or cold or hungry. She drops all the heavy words like: "This is not fair", or "This is not my job". She hears only the beat of her wings and she is grateful

and happy they are the right kind to get her there.'

'Do you think you have to be brave to fly so far?'

'You find the courage along the way. Sometimes, little one, being brave is having no other choices left.'

'Look, Baba Didi! Look! They're leaving!'

The godwits were lifting off the beach. Hanging in the wind, practising. The birds lifted like crumbs scattered off a picnic rug and swirled in a mass above them.

Isabella closed her eyes and twirled beneath them and saw… the lighthouse at tip of Cape Reinga where the two oceans meet! She saw the marshes of North Korea and the swamps of South China. And now she was landing – landing with the other godwits, a stranger, surrounded by the fluttering and bickering of other strange birds. Isabella blinked.

'Where were you?' said Baba Didi. 'Help me get these pipis on my back will you, love?'

Isabella helped Baba Didi settle the bag of pipis on her back. The godwits were still lifting in groups off the beach, hanging for a minute and then slowly, steadily, flying out to sea.

'Say hello to Japan and Korea! Russia and Alaska too! Say hi to China!' Isabella and Baba Didi watched until the first group were small dots over the waves.

'Goodbye godwits!' yelled Isabella, 'I hope you find lots of good things to eat! We'll be waiting for you when the sea worms are juicy and fat next spring!'

Baba Didi and Isabella waved and waved until those small nuggety birds were out of sight.

'I'm tired,' said Isabella.

'Pah!' said Baba Didi. 'Have I been talking to the wind? Where is your godwit spirit? Show me those godwit wings! Mine are old but they are still good.'

With that, Baba Didi went running with her dodgy hip down the beach, flapping her arms like wings and laughing.

And Isabella went running after.